RECORD BREAKERS

FOOTBALL

Blaine Wiseman

www.av2books.com

AV² by Weigl brings you media enhanced books that support active learning.

AV² provides enriched content that supplements and complements this book. Weigl's AV² books strive to create inspired learning and engage young minds for a total learning experience.

Go to **www.av2books.com**, and enter this book's unique code. You will have access to video, audio, web links, quizzes, a slide show, and activities.

BOOK CODE

G 4 1 3 2 0 1

Audio
Listen to sections of the book read aloud.

Video
Watch informative video clips.

Web Link
Find research sites and play interactive games.

Try This!
Complete activities and hands-on experiments.

Due to the dynamic nature of the Internet, some of the URLs and activities provided as part of AV² by Weigl may have changed or ceased to exist. AV² by Weigl accepts no responsibility for any such changes. All media enhanced books are regularly monitored to update addresses and sites in a timely manner. Contact AV² by Weigl at 1-866-649-3445 or av2books@weigl.com with any questions, comments, or feedback.

Published by AV² by Weigl
350 5th Avenue, 59th Floor
New York, NY 10118
Website: www.av2books.com   www.weigl.com

Library of Congress Cataloging-in-Publication Data available upon request.
Fax 1-866-44-WEIGL for the attention of the Publishing Records department.

ISBN 978-1-61690-103-5 (hard cover)
ISBN 978-1-61690-104-2 (soft cover)

Printed in the United States of America in North Mankato, Minnesota
1 2 3 4 5 6 7 8 9 0 14 13 12 11 10

052010
WEP264000

Project Coordinator Heather C. Hudak
Design Terry Paulhus

Contents

The Offense

Brett Favre has broken many NFL quarterback records. He is known for his dedication to winning and his excellent play in cold weather. Here are some of Favre's records.

Most consecutive starts by a quarterback – 271

Most regular season wins by a starting quarterback – 160
John Elway is second with 148.

Most career passing touchdowns – 497
Dan Marino is second with 420.

Most career passing yards – 69,329
Marino is second with 61,361 passing yards in his career.

Most career pass completions – 6,083
Marino is second with 4,967 completions.

Most career games with three or more touchdowns – 63
Marino is second with 62 games.

Jason Elam

Kick It

Kickers play an important role on a football team. They only work for a few seconds at a time, but kickers are under a great deal of pressure. The record for the longest field goal ever kicked is shared by Tom Dempsey and Jason Elam. Dempsey, who was born with no toes on his kicking foot, made his 63-yard kick for the New Orleans Saints in 1970. Elam equaled Dempsey's kick while playing for the Denver Broncos in 1998.

Brett Favre

Pigskin Pioneers

Many of the best football players have been African American. In 1902, Charles W. Follis became the first African American to play **professional** football. He played for the Shelby Athletic Club.

When the National Football League (NFL) began in 1920, there were only two African American players in the league. They were Fritz Pollard and Bobby Marshall. Pollard, a back, led the Akron Pros to the first league championship. The next year, he became the first professional African American football coach.

The first African American quarterback in the NFL was Willie Thrower. He threw the ball for the Chicago Bears in 1953.

The first time an African American head coach led his team to the Super Bowl was in 2006. That year, both coaches in the Super Bowl were African American. Tony Dungy's Indianapolis Colts beat Lovie Smith's Chicago Bears 29 to 17. Dungy became the first African American coach to win the Super Bowl.

Emmitt Smith

Running Game

Running backs carry the ball down the field, dodging tackles, jumping over defenders, and spinning away from blocks. It is a running back's job to gain as many yards as possible, using speed, strength, and skill. Emmitt Smith has run for more yards than any other running back.

During his career, Smith ran for 18,355 yards. He also scored more rushing touchdowns than any other player, with 164 rushing touchdowns. LaDainian Tomlinson, who plays for the San Diego Chargers, is in second place with 138 rushing touchdowns.

Shaun Alexander, running back

The Defense

Football players often are tackled by several players who weigh more than 300 pounds (136 kilograms) each. These are some of the biggest football players in history.

Aaron Gibson – Tackle, 2006 Buffalo Bills
Height and Weight: 6 feet 6 inches (1.98 meters) and 410 pounds (186 kg)

Langston Walker – Tackle, 2009 Oakland Raiders
Height and Weight: 6 feet 8 inches (2 m) and 360 pounds (163 kg)

Leonard Davis – Guard, 2009 Dallas Cowboys
Height and Weight: 6 feet 6 inches (1.98 m) and 353 pounds (160 kg)

Grady Jackson – Tackle, 2009 Detroit Lions
Height and Weight: 6 feet 2 inches (1.88 m) and 345 pounds (156.5 kg)

Joe Greene

The Wall

Defensive lines are made up of players whose job it is to prevent the other team from moving upfield. The best defensive line in NFL history belongs to the Pittsburgh Steelers. During the 1970s, the "Steel Curtain" was led by "Mean" Joe Greene. The team won four Super Bowls in six years, dominating with defense. These are some other great defensive lines.

The Fearsome Foursome
Los Angeles Rams, 1960s and 1970s

The Purple People Eaters
Minnesota Vikings, 1960s and 1970s

The New York Sack Exchange
New York Jets, 1980s

Aaron Gibson

Ed Reed

Interceptors

One of the most exciting plays in football is an interception. An interception happens when a defensive player catches a ball thrown by the other team's quarterback. One interception can change the outcome of a football game. Here are some of the records for interceptions.

Most career interceptions – 81
Player: Paul Krause
Teams: Washington Redskins, 1964–1967
Minnesota Vikings, 1968–1979

Most interceptions in one season – 14
Player: Dick "Night Train" Lane
Team: Los Angeles Rams, 1952

Most career interceptions yards gained – 1483
Player: Rod Woodson
Teams: Pittsburgh Steelers, 1987–1996
San Francisco 49ers, 1997
Baltimore Ravens, 1998–2001
Oakland Raiders, 2002–2003

Most career interceptions touchdowns – 12
Player: Rod Woodson
Teams: Pittsburgh Steelers, 1987–1996
San Francisco 49ers, 1997
Baltimore Ravens, 1998–2001
Oakland Raiders, 2002–2003

Longest interception return – 106 yards
Player: Ed Reed
Team: Baltimore Ravens, 2004

Sack Attack

The quarterback is the most important player on the field. The offensive line protects the quarterback from the other team's defense. The act of tackling the quarterback before he makes a play is called a sack. Bruce Smith was able to break through the offensive line for 200 quarterback sacks in his career with the Buffalo Bills and Washington Redskins. In Smith's final season in the NFL, he broke Reggie White's record of 198 sacks.

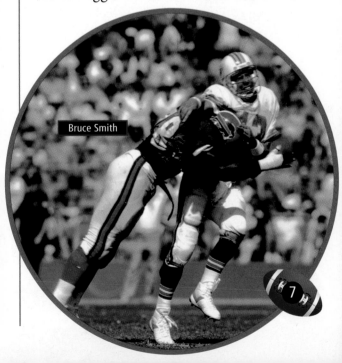
Bruce Smith

7

Special Strategies

> "Football is an incredible game. Sometimes it's so incredible, it's unbelievable."
>
> – Tom Landry

Tom Landry

Bill Parcells

Coaching Champions

Only 12 coaches have won more than one Super Bowl. Of these, only seven have never lost in the Super Bowl.

Coach/Team	Wins	Losses
Don Shula		
Baltimore Colts	0	1
Miami Dolphins	2	3
Tom Landry		
Dallas Cowboys	2	3
Chuck Noll		
Pittsburgh Steelers	4	0
Bill Parcells		
New York Giants	2	0
New England Patriots	0	1
Joe Gibbs		
Washington Redskins	3	1
Mike Shanahan		
Denver Broncos	2	0
Bill Belichick		
New England Patriots	3	1
George Seifert		
San Francisco 49ers	2	0
Bill Walsh		
San Francisco 49ers	3	0
Vince Lombardi		
Green Bay Packers	2	0
Tom Flores		
Oakland/Los Angeles Raiders	2	0
Jimmy Johnson		
Dallas Cowboys	2	0

Dolphin Don

Don Shula is the most successful NFL head coach. Shula's career as a head coach began with the Baltimore Colts in 1963 and lasted until he retired from the Miami Dolphins in 1995. He holds several records and has coached the only perfect season in NFL history. During the 1972 season, Shula's Miami Dolphins won all 17 of their games. The Dolphins beat the Washington Redskins 14 to 7 in Super Bowl VII that season. Shula's teams made the playoffs 20 times in 33 years. His teams won at least 10 games in a season 21 times. These are some of Shula's accomplishments.

Most wins by a head coach – 347
He only lost 173 games.

Most Super Bowl appearances by a head coach – 6
Shula won the Super Bowl twice.

At the time, youngest coach ever – 33 years
Since then, seven younger coaches, including Shula's son, David, have worked in the NFL.

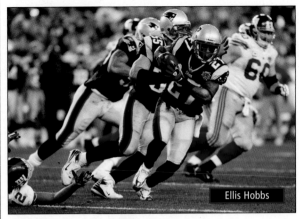
Ellis Hobbs

Many Happy Returns

Special teams are an important part of football. These "teams" are made up of players who are on the field for kicking plays. Kicking plays include kickoffs, field goals, and punts. During kickoffs and punts, one player catches the ball and tries to return it to the other team's end zone. A successful kick return is one of the most exciting plays in football. Some players have made great careers out of returning kicks.

Most career kick and punt return yards – 19,013
Player: Brian Mitchell
Teams: Washington Redskins 1990–1999
Philadelphia Eagles, 2000–2002
New York Giants, 2003

Most career kick return touchdowns – 8
Player: Josh Cribs
Team: Cleveland Browns, 2005–Present

Longest kick return – 108 yards
Player: Ellis Hobbs
Team: New England Patriots, 2007

Don Shula

The Super Bowl

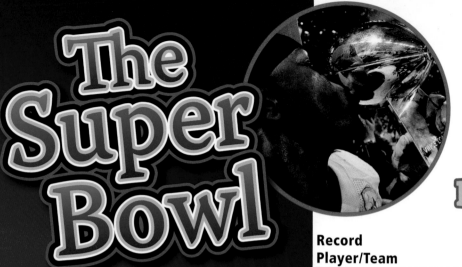

Record Player/Team	Year(s) Won
Most wins by a team – 6	
Pittsburgh Steelers	1975, 1976, 1979, 1980, 2006, 2009
Most wins – coach	
Chuck Noll, Pittsburgh Steelers	1975, 1976, 1979, 1980
Most Super Bowl MVPs – 3	
Joe Montana (QB), San Francisco 49ers	1985, 1989, 1990
Most Career Touchdowns – 8	
Jerry Rice (WR), San Francisco 49ers Oakland Raiders	1989, 1990, 1995 2003

Sizing It Up

The Vince Lombardi Trophy is the best-known award in football. The handmade, 22-inch (55.9-centimeter) tall trophy is made by Tiffany & Co. in New York City. Each year, the trophy is presented to the owner of the Super Bowl winning team. The trophy is a **sterling** silver football sitting on a base that is **engraved** with the words "Vince Lombardi Trophy" and the NFL logo. Though the trophy weighs only 7 pounds (3.2 kg), the entire team lifts it. It is considered priceless to football players despite the fact that it is only valued at $12,500.

Name Game

The Super Bowl began in 1966 as a game between the champions of the NFL and the American Football League (AFL). The event was known as the AFL/NFL Championship Game. The first championship team was the NFL's Green Bay Packers, coached by Vince Lombardi, who ended up winning Super Bowls I and II. In 1970, Lombardi was the coach for the Washington Redskins when he died of cancer. The Super Bowl trophy was named after him in 1971. Many people consider Lombardi the greatest coach of all time. He was known for his dedication to the sport, as well as many memorable quotes. Here are some of Lombardi's quotes.

Vince Lombardi

"ONCE YOU LEARN TO QUIT, IT BECOMES A HABIT."

"IT'S NOT WHETHER YOU GET KNOCKED DOWN, IT'S WHETHER YOU GET UP."

"WINNING ISN'T EVERYTHING, BUT WANTING TO WIN IS."

So Close

Three teams are tied for most losses in Super Bowl history. The Buffalo Bills, Denver Broncos, and Minnesota Vikings have each lost four championship games. The Broncos finally achieved their championship dream by winning the Super Bowl in 1998 and 1999. The Vikings and Bills have never won the Vince Lombardi Trophy. From 1991 to 1994, the Bills lost in the final game, four straight years. No other team has lost more than two Super Bowl games in a row.

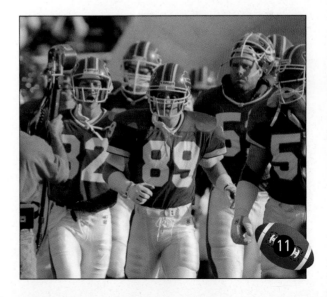

The Gear

The Pads

In football, players collide at high speeds. In the early days of the sport, there were few rules, and football players did not wear padding. Injuries were common. President Theodore Roosevelt threatened to ban football due to the violent nature of the game. In 1910, rule changes and the use of padding, such as shoulder pads and helmets, made football safer.

The Pigskin

The first footballs were made hundreds of years ago in the 11th century. The balls were made from a pig's **bladder**. Bladders are round and were inflated with air to form a ball. In the 1870s, pigs' bladders were replaced with rubber bladders. The rubber bladders were covered with leather. In 1935, the leather football was made smaller and slimmer. This design is still used in the NFL today.

Larry Johnson

Watch Your Head

In 1893, Navy Admiral Joseph Mason Reeves was the first person to wear a helmet for football. He had hit his head playing football, and a doctor told Reeves that he could die if he was kicked in the head again. Reeves' helmet was made by a shoemaker, and he wore it during a game against the army.

The first NFL team to paint a logo on their helmet was the Los Angeles Rams in 1948. Today, many teams display their colors and logo on their helmets.

Black Eyes

Football players are known for painting black stripes below their eyes. The stripes reduce the Sun's glare, helping the players see better. In 1942, Andy Farkas of the Washington Redskins became the first player to paint on the stripes. At first, players smeared shoe polish or burnt cork on their cheeks. Today, they can buy black grease or stickers.

Get a Grip

Football players wear shoes called cleats. They have spikes, or pieces of plastic, on the bottom. This helps their feet grip the ground so they do not slip on grass or turf.

Converse created the first football shoe in 1917. The shoes were decorated with the United States flag. Before that, soccer shoes were used. The first modern football shoe was Puma's Atom. The shoe came out in 1948, and it looked much like today's football shoes, featuring cleats and a formed sole.

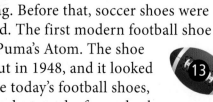

13

More Records

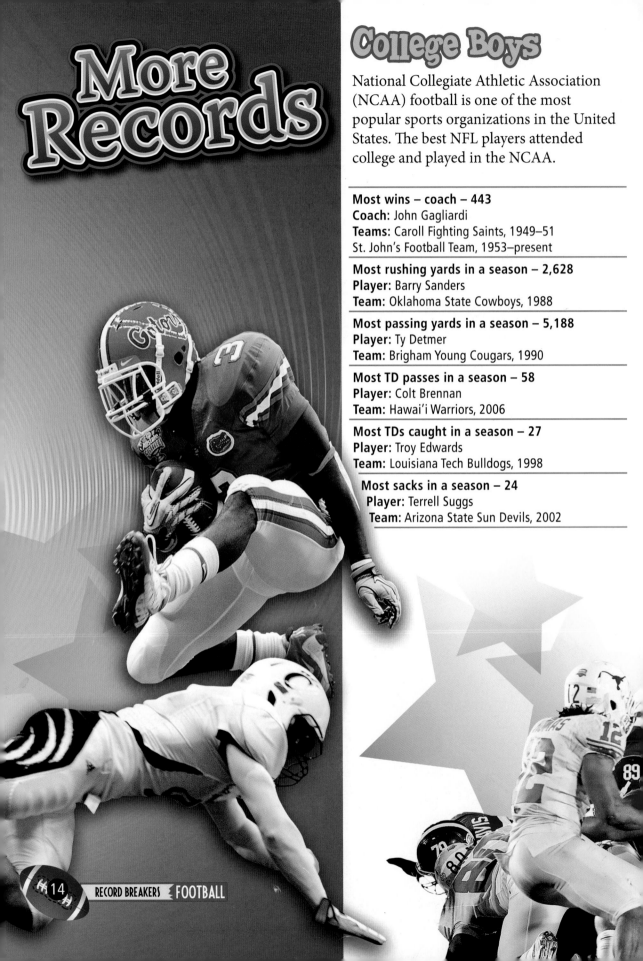

College Boys

National Collegiate Athletic Association (NCAA) football is one of the most popular sports organizations in the United States. The best NFL players attended college and played in the NCAA.

Most wins – coach – 443
Coach: John Gagliardi
Teams: Caroll Fighting Saints, 1949–51
St. John's Football Team, 1953–present

Most rushing yards in a season – 2,628
Player: Barry Sanders
Team: Oklahoma State Cowboys, 1988

Most passing yards in a season – 5,188
Player: Ty Detmer
Team: Brigham Young Cougars, 1990

Most TD passes in a season – 58
Player: Colt Brennan
Team: Hawai'i Warriors, 2006

Most TDs caught in a season – 27
Player: Troy Edwards
Team: Louisiana Tech Bulldogs, 1998

Most sacks in a season – 24
Player: Terrell Suggs
Team: Arizona State Sun Devils, 2002

College Girls

The first woman to play in an NCAA football game was Katie Hnida. On Christmas Day in 2002, Hnida kicked an extra point for the New Mexico Lobos. The kick was blocked, but Hnida had made history. The next season, she became the first female to score a point in the NCAA, kicking two extra points.

Katie Hnida

The First Game

The first American football game was a college match between Rutgers and Princeton in 1869. Rutgers wanted revenge against its rivals after the Princeton baseball team had beat the Rutgers team by a score of 40 to 2. The football teams each had 25 players, and the rules were different from those of today. The ball could not be carried or thrown. It could only be kicked or hit down the field. Rutgers achieved its goal, winning the football game 6 to 4.

Most Valuable Players

Each year, the Associated Press awards one football player the title Most Valuable Player. The players on this map have won this honor more times than any other players in the NFL.

Kurt Warner

MVP 2 Times

Born: Burlington, Iowa
Position: Quarterback
MVP: 1999, 2001
Team: St. Louis Rams

Pacific Ocean

Steve Young

MVP 2 Times

Born: Salt Lake City, Utah
Position: Quarterback
MVP: 1992, 1994
Team: San Francisco 49ers

Peyton Manning

MVP 4 Times

Born: New Orleans, Louisiana
Position: Quarterback
MVP: 2003,2004, 2008,2009
Team: Indianapolis Colts

Joe Montana

MVP 2 Times

Born:
New Eagle, Pennsylvania
Position: Quarterback
MVP: 1989, 1990
Team: San Francisco 49ers

Johnny Unitas

MVP 3 Times

Born:
Pittsburgh, Pennsylvania
Position: Quarterback
MVP: 1959, 1964, 1967
Team: Baltimore Colts

Jim Brown

MVP 3 Times

Born:
St. Simons Island, Georgia
Position: Fullback
MVP: 1957, 1958, 1965
Team: Cleveland Browns

Brett Favre

MVP 3 Times

Born:
Gulfport, Mississippi
Position: Quarterback
MVP: 1995, 1996, 1997
Team: Green Bay Packers

UNITED
STATES

Atlantic

Ocean

N
W E
S

140 Miles
0 225 Kilometers

17

The Stadiums

Everything's Bigger in Texas

The Original

The oldest stadium in the NFL is Lambeau Field in Green Bay, Wisconsin. The Packers have played at Lambeau Field since 1957. They have won four Super Bowls and become one of the most successful teams in NFL history. Lambeau Field is home to the Lambeau Leap, a tradition that has players jump into the crowd after scoring a touchdown.

In 2009, the Dallas Cowboys began their season in the new Cowboys Stadium, the largest stadium in the NFL. The stadium can hold more than 100,000 fans for Cowboys' games and cost $1.15 billion to build. The **retractable** roof is the largest in the world and takes 12 minutes to open or close. The largest screen in the world hangs above the field. Two additional screens that measure 72 feet (22 meters) tall and 160 feet (48.8 m) wide face the sidelines, while 28 by 50 foot (8.5 by 15.2 m) screens face the end zones.

The Biggest Barns

Cowboys Stadium
Team – Dallas Cowboys
Seats – 105,121

FedEx Field
Team – Washington Redskins
Seats – 91,704

Meadowlands Stadium
Teams – New York Giants and Jets
Seats – 82,500

Arrowhead Stadium
Team – Kansas City Chiefs
Seats – 79,101

Jacksonville Municipal Stadium
Team – Jacksonville Jaguars
Seats – 78,867

Catching Rays

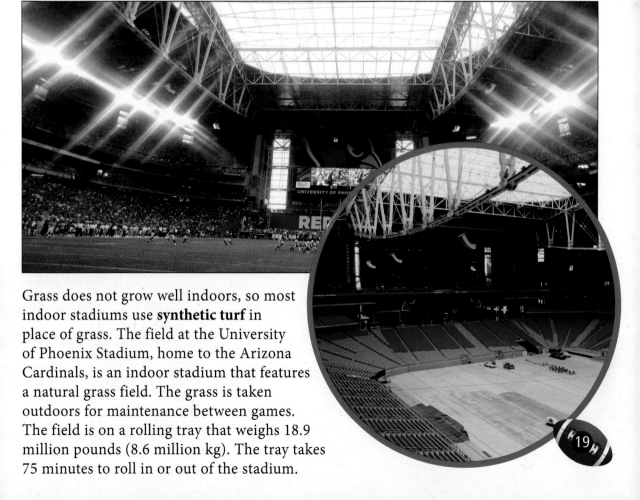

Grass does not grow well indoors, so most indoor stadiums use **synthetic turf** in place of grass. The field at the University of Phoenix Stadium, home to the Arizona Cardinals, is an indoor stadium that features a natural grass field. The grass is taken outdoors for maintenance between games. The field is on a rolling tray that weighs 18.9 million pounds (8.6 million kg). The tray takes 75 minutes to roll in or out of the stadium.

In The Money

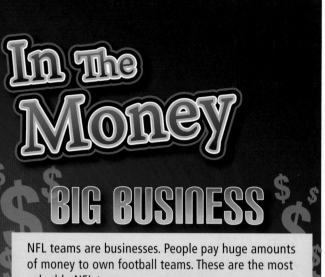

BIG BUSINESS

NFL teams are businesses. People pay huge amounts of money to own football teams. These are the most valuable NFL teams.

Dallas Cowboys - $1.7 billion

Washington Redskins - $1.6 billion

New England Patriots - $1.4 billion

New York Giants - $1.2 billion

New York Jets - $1.2 billion

Funding the Game

On average, how much do people spend at an NFL game?
Ticket: $ 75
Hot dog: $ 4.50
Soft drink: $ 4
Program: $ 4.50
Hat: $16

Sporting Salaries

NFL players are highly paid. The minimum salary in the NFL is $310,000, while the best players make millions of dollars each year. These are the highest-paid football players in the world, excluding **sponsorship** deals.

Philip Rivers
San Diego Chargers - $25.5 million

Donovan McNabb
Philadelphia Eagles - $25 million

Eli Manning
New York Giants - $20.5 million

Chris Long
St. Louis Rams - $19.1 million

Kurt Warner
Arizona Cardinals - $19 million

Culture

The Dawg Pound

The Dawg Pound is the name given to a section of the Cleveland Browns' stadium behind the end zone. The fans in this section are well-known for their support of the Browns. When the Browns moved to Baltimore in 1996, Browns fans were upset. After three years of **protests** and **petitions**, the Browns returned to Cleveland in 1999. The Dawg Pound is alive and strong today because of the dedicated fans who refused to lose their team.

Mascots

Many NFL teams have mascots that help excite the fans by running around the stadium during games. Mascots often lead the team onto the field to start the game. The Minnesota Vikings mascot, Ragnar, is a motorcycle riding Viking with fur clothes and a horned helmet.

Super Fans

Football fans are known for their passion and dedication to the game and the home team. They gather before the games in stadium parking lots, enjoying hamburgers and hot dogs, talking with other football fans, and **tailgating**. They brave cold weather, rain, and snow to support their football heroes. In some cities, fans take part in special traditions. Green Bay Packers fans are known as Cheeseheads. They wear bright yellow, foam cheesehead hats to celebrate Wisconsin's dairy industry. Oakland Raiders fans dress in the team's colors, black and silver.

QUIZ

1 Who was the first African-American quarterback in the NFL?

2 Who is the heaviest player in NFL history?

3 What coach won 347 NFL games?

4 Who is the Super Bowl trophy named after?

5 What team lost in four straight Super Bowls?

6 What were footballs originally made of?

7 Who was the first woman to score in an NCAA football game?

8 What player has been given the most MVP awards?

9 What is the most valuable NFL team?

10 What is the name given to Green Bay Packers fans?

ANSWERS: 1. Willie Thrower 2. Aaron Gibson 3. Don Shula 4. Vince Lombardi 5. The Buffalo Bills 6. Pigs' bladders 7. Katie Hnida 8. Peyton Manning 9. The Dallas Cowboys 10. Cheeseheads

GLOSSARY

bladder: an organ inside the body that collects and disposes of urine

engraved: carved into the surface

petitions: written requests signed by many people

professional: paid to play

protests: actions to show disapproval

regular season: the 17 weeks of games leading up to the playoffs

retractable: can be opened or closed

sponsorship: money paid to a person by a company in exchange for advertising

sterling: high-quality silver

synthetic turf: a surface of human-made materials that resembles grass

tailgating: partying in a parking lot

INDEX

Log on to www.av2books.com

AV² by Weigl brings you media enhanced books that support active learning. Go to **www.av2books.com**, and enter the special code inside the front cover of this book. You will gain access to enriched and enhanced content that supplements and complements this book. Content includes video, audio, web links, quizzes, a slide show, and activities.

Audio
Listen to sections of the book read aloud.

Video
Watch informative video clips.

Web Link
Find research sites and play interactive games.

Try This!
Complete activities and hands-on experiments.

WHAT'S ONLINE?

Try This!
Complete activities and hands-on experiments.

Pages 10-11 Try this football activity.

Pages 12-13 Test your knowledge of football gear.

Pages 16-17 Complete this mapping activity.

Web Link
Find research sites and play interactive games.

Pages 6-7 Learn more about football players.

Pages 8-9 Read about football coaches.

Pages 18-19 Find out more about where football games take place.

Video
Watch informative video clips.

Pages 4-5 Watch a video about football.

Pages 14-15 View stars of the sport in action.

Pages 20-21 Watch a video about football players.

EXTRA FEATURES

Audio
Hear introductory au at the top of every p

Key Words
Study vocabulary, and play a matching word game.

Slide Show
View images and captions, and try a writing activity.

AV² Quiz
Take this quiz to test your knowledge

Due to the dynamic nature of the Internet, some of the URLs and activities provided as part of AV² by Weigl may have changed or ceased to exist. AV² by Weigl accepts no responsibility for any such changes. All media enhanced books are regularly monitored to update addresses and sites in a timely manner. Contact AV² by Weigl at 1-866-649-3445 c av2books@weigl.com with any questions, comments, or feedback.